Y0-CPD-876

TELL ME WHY
Earth is like
a jigsaw puzzle

Barbara Taylor

KINGFISHER

NEW YORK

KINGFISHER
LONDON & NEW YORK

Copyright © Kingfisher 2013
Published in the United States by Kingfisher,
175 Fifth Ave., New York, NY 10010
Kingfisher is an imprint of
Macmillan Children's Books, London.
All rights reserved.

Concept by Ray Bryant
Designed and illustrated by Dynamo Design

Distributed in the U.S. and Canada by Macmillan,
175 Fifth Ave., New York, NY 10010

Library of Congress Cataloging-in-Publication data
has been applied for.

ISBN: 978-0-7534-7085-5

Kingfisher books are available for special promotions and premiums.
For details contact: Special Markets Department, Macmillan,
175 Fifth Ave., New York, NY 10010.

For more information, please visit www.kingfisherbooks.com

Printed in China
2 4 6 8 9 7 5 3 1
1TR/0413/WKT/UG/128MA

Contents

Tell me why...

Earth needs a blanket

The thin blanket of gases around Earth shields it from the Sun's harmful rays and from meteors. It also stops Earth from getting too hot or too cold. This blanket is called the atmosphere, and life on Earth could not exist without it. Living things need to breathe the air in the atmosphere to stay alive. The atmosphere becomes thinner (contains less air) farther away from Earth, which is why it is hard for climbers to breathe high up on mountains.

If you could look at Earth from a spaceship, you would see the atmosphere as a thin, blue haze around the planet.

Uncovered Moon

The Moon does not have an atmosphere because the pulling force of its gravity is too weak to hold any gases around it. Earth's gravity is much stronger and so holds its blanket of gases in place.

5

Tell me why...
it gets dark at night

Earth is a spinning ball of rock that takes one day and one night (24 hours) to turn around once. When your part of Earth turns away from the Sun, the Sun's light cannot reach you, so it gets dark. This is when you have nighttime. When your part of Earth turns around to face the Sun again, sunlight can reach you once more, so you have daytime. While you are having breakfast, people on the other side of the world are going to sleep!

Surprising Sun

The Sun seems to rise in the sky during the day and sink down again at night, but it is actually the movement of Earth that causes this. As Earth spins around, it makes the Sun appear to rise and set.

In places near the North and South poles, the Sun stays low in the sky at night for six months of the year. So for half of the year it is light at night there.

Tell me why...
some places have four seasons

The four seasons of spring, summer, fall, and winter are regular changes in the pattern of the weather. These seasons happen because Earth is tilted at an angle as it moves around the Sun. In the spring and summer Earth is tilted toward the Sun, so the weather is warmer, with long, bright days. In the fall and winter Earth is tilted away from the Sun, so the weather is colder, with shorter days and long, dark nights.

Hibernation

Some animals, such as marmots and bats, survive the long, cold winter months by retreating into their cave or burrow and going into a very deep sleep. This is called hibernation.

Animals that hibernate, such as this dormouse, eat a lot in the fall and use stored body fat to stay alive during their winter sleep.

7

Tell me why...

Earth has a cold top and bottom

The polar lands at the top and bottom of Earth are cold because Earth's surface is curved. The Sun's rays have to travel farther through Earth's atmosphere to reach these lands, and they are weaker when they arrive. The rays are also spread out over Earth's curved surface, which reduces their heating power. All the white ice and snow in polar lands makes them even colder. This is because the white color reflects most of the Sun's rays, so the heat bounces back into the sky.

Hot waist

Around the middle of Earth—its "waist"—the Sun's rays hit the planet straight on and its heat is concentrated, making it very hot in this region. The green plants that grow there reflect only 20 percent of the Sun's heat.

Many kinds of penguins live in the cold lands at the bottom of Earth. Often, penguins huddle together in big groups to share warmth, taking turns standing in the middle.

Tell me why...
some mountains breathe fire

Red-hot liquid rock from deep inside Earth sometimes bursts through cracks in the surface to produce fountains of fire. This helps cool the center of Earth, which is incredibly hot. On the surface, the liquid rock cools down into solid rock and forms mountains called volcanoes. The red-hot rock may be pushed up to the surface by bubbles of gas. The bubbles in a bottle of soda can make the liquid spray out of the top of the bottle in a similar way.

The hot rock that explodes out of a volcano can be ten times hotter than boiling water! It slides along at speeds of up to 590 feet (180 meters) per second.

Hot baths

Hot rock sometimes heats up underground water, which rises to the surface to form bubbling hot springs. In the mountains of Japan, macaque monkeys often take baths in hot springs to stay warm in the winter.

11

Tell me why...

Earth is like a jigsaw puzzle

The surface of Earth is like a giant jigsaw puzzle because it is made up of pieces—called plates—that fit together. There are about 14 large plates and 38 smaller ones. Most plates contain some of Earth's continents (big areas of land) and some of the ocean floor. Hot rocks churning around inside Earth make the plates slip and slide around. This makes the continents move around, so they are in different places today than they were millions of years ago.

Creeping continents

The way continents move around on the surface of Earth is known as continental drift. They drift only a few inches every year, though, which is about the same speed as your fingernails grow.

The Himalayas formed when the plate carrying India pushed into the one carrying the rest of Asia. The rocks in between the two plates were pushed up to make mountains.

Tell me why...
Earth shakes and cracks open

When energy stored in underground rocks is suddenly released at a weak point in Earth's surface, an earthquake happens, making the ground tremble and shake. Sometimes the surface splits apart along a jagged line called a fault, as huge blocks of rock slide past one another or move up or down. The biggest earthquakes are caused by plate movements and can destroy buildings and bridges. In some areas where earthquakes happen a lot, buildings are built to be "earthquake proof." They are flexible and have strong foundations, so they do not crumble when the ground shakes.

Giant waves

If an earthquake happens under the ocean, it can trigger a giant wave called a tsunami (soo-naam-ee). Tsunamis can travel at speeds of up to 500 miles (800 kilometers) per hour and reach heights of about 100 feet (30 meters) near the coast.

Many buildings were destroyed in the big San Francisco earthquake of 1989, which lasted only 10–15 seconds. It was caused by rocks sliding past one another along the San Andreas fault line.

Tell me why...
there are chimneys in the ocean

Superhot seawater, heated by volcanic rock deep within Earth's crust, can spout out of cracks called vents on the ocean floor. The superheated water contains lot of minerals, which drop out in the cold seawater on the ocean floor. The minerals stick together and build up to form tall chimneys. As the hot water flows up through the chimneys, it turns the water black or white, making them look like real chimneys with smoke pouring out of the top!

This smoking "chimney" is thousands of feet below the surface of the sea on the floor of the Pacific Ocean. The chimney is covered with giant tube worms.

Creatures of the deep

Unusual creatures live in the dark around the chimneys. There are giant tube worms 3 feet (1 meter) long, blind shrimp, sea snails, octopuses, and giant clams as big as dinner plates!

Tell me why...
rain falls from the sky

The rain that falls from the sky starts off as water on the ground. The Sun heats the water, turning it into an invisible gas called water vapor. The water vapor rises up into the sky, where it cools down and turns back into tiny drops of water again. Billions of water drops collect together to form clouds that float in the sky. When the clouds are heavy enough, the water drops fall down to the ground as rain. Rain clouds often look gray because they are so full of water that light can't shine through them.

Cloud shapes

Clouds come in different shapes and sizes. Wispy ice clouds float high up in the sky. Fluffy cumulus clouds look like cotton balls but can grow into giant thunderstorm clouds. Flat stratus clouds cover the sky in a gray comforter.

These are storm clouds gathering over the city of Kiev, Ukraine. They are called cumulonimbus clouds—cumulus means "heap" and nimbus means "cloud."

Tell me why...
rainbows are so colorful

Rainbows show us the colors in sunlight that are usually hidden from our eyes. As light shines through raindrops, the water makes the colors spread out so that we can see each one by itself. From the ground, a rainbow is shaped like an arch, but if you look down from a plane, it is possible to see a circular rainbow! We all see a slightly different rainbow because of the way the sunlight bounces off the raindrops into our eyes.

Moonbow
If the Moon shines brightly through the rain, it may create a rainbow at night! These are called moonbows, but they are very rare and difficult to photograph.

Rainbows also appear when the Sun shines through the drops of water spraying from a waterfall. This photo shows a rainbow at Niagara Falls.

17

Tell me why...

the sky roars and flashes

Thunder and lightning happen when a sudden burst of electricity escapes from tall storm clouds. This static electricity is created when water droplets and ice crystals are tossed up and down inside the clouds by strong air currents so that they rub against one another. Eventually, the built-up energy is released as a flash of lightning, which zigzags down to the ground or jumps between clouds. The sparks of lightning are so hot that they make the air suddenly spread out and shake at great speed, producing a loud crash of thunder.

Lightning jumps down to the ground and back up to the clouds again along the same path. If lightning strikes a tree, it can set it on fire.

Counting game

To find out how far away a storm is in miles, count the seconds between the lightning and the thunder and divide by 5. (For kilometers, divide the number of seconds by 2.5.) Lightning and thunder happen at the same time, but you see the lightning before you hear the thunder because light travels much faster than sound.

Tell me why . . .

the sky is blue

Sunlight is made up of many different colors of light. When it reaches Earth's atmosphere, the different colors of light are scattered in all directions by gases and particles in the air. But the blue light is scattered more than the other colors because it travels a shorter distance. This means that when you look at the sky on a clear day, you see more of the blue parts of light—and so the sky appears blue.

Black sky

Space looks black because there are no particles there to scatter the colors in sunlight. The sunlight travels in straight lines and we cannot see the colors that we see in the sky on Earth.

Clouds are white because they scatter the colors of light in every direction. All the colors combine to produce white light.

20

Tell me why...
sunsets are red

When the Sun begins to set, it is lower in the sky and its rays have to travel through more of Earth's atmosphere before reaching you. More of the light bounces off particles in the air and is scattered. All of the colors are scattered too far away from Earth to be seen, except for red and orange. The red and orange colors are the only ones to reach your eyes, so the sky looks red as the Sun sets beneath the horizon.

Super sunsets

The tiny particles of dust and gas thrown high into the sky by volcanoes sometimes cause spectacular sunsets. The extra particles scatter most of the colors away and only the deep reds remain to reach your eyes.

Sunsets are more colorful than sunrises because the air is usually more still in the morning, so there are fewer particles of dust around for the red and orange light to bounce off.

Tell me why...
the tide comes in and goes out

Tides are the way the ocean moves up and down the beach every day. At high tide, the ocean is close to the top of the beach. At low tide the ocean is close to the bottom of the beach. There are usually two high tides and two low tides every day. Tides happen because the Moon and the Sun pull Earth's oceans toward them with a force called gravity. The Moon's gravity is the main pulling force because it is much closer to Earth than the Sun is.

The difference between the high and low tides in Canada's Bay of Fundy is as much as 52 feet (16 meters)! This is because of the unique size and shape of the bay.

Spring tides

Spring tides are higher and lower than normal tides. They happen twice a month, when the Sun, Moon, and Earth are all lined up. The pull of the Sun and the pull of the Moon combine to make a superstrong tugging force at these times.

Tell me why...
caves form underground

When rainwater drains down through the cracks in limestone rocks, it eats into the soft rocks, carving out big, underground rooms called caves. The rainwater contains acids, which break up the rocks into tiny pieces. These pieces of rock disappear into the water and are washed away in rivers that flow underground. Less than an inch (only a few millimeters) of limestone is washed away in a year, so it can take thousands of years for large caves to form.

The incredible decorations inside Carlsbad Caverns in New Mexico make them look like wedding cakes! They formed when billions of drops of water deposited minerals they were carrying to form rocky icicles, pillars, and domes.

Cave creatures

Many cave creatures, such as cave fish, are blind because their eyes are no use in the dark. They rely instead on their senses of touch and smell to find their way around and to locate food.

Tell me why...
some rocks contain crystals

Crystals grow inside rocks when the minerals that make up the rocks have enough space to grow into their natural geometric shape. This often happens when liquid rock from deep inside Earth cools and hardens. Sometimes, heat and pressure underground concentrate minerals in pockets of rock or very hot water. Then the minerals cool to form crystals. Crystals can be cut and polished to form sparkling gemstones.

Slow growth

Most mineral crystals take thousands of years to grow. The largest crystals form very slowly, taking up to 2,200 years to grow just one millimeter!

These giant crystals are the biggest in the world! They are in a Mexican cave 985 feet (300 meters) underground. People have to wear backpacks of ice-cold air to stay alive inside the very hot, damp cave.

Tell me why...

dinosaurs are hiding in the rocks

Living dinosaurs are not actually lurking in the rocks, waiting to jump out and surprise you! However, the remains of many dinosaurs that died millions of years ago are still trapped in the rocks of our planet. They are preserved as stone fossils. From dinosaur fossils, scientists can figure out things such as how big they were, what they ate, how fast they moved, how they took care of their babies, and even how they communicated with one another.

Dinosaur footprints, preserved in the rock, tell us how many toes dinosaurs had on their feet. This one was probably a meat eater that walked on two legs.

Dinosaur feathers

Fossils of some small, meat-eating dinosaurs show that they had wings and feathers. They used their feathers for warmth and display (to help find a mate), and some could even glide on their feathered wings.

Tell me why...
rainforests are like coral reefs

Rainforests and coral reefs are home to the greatest variety of living things on planet Earth. They are warm environments with plenty of food for animals to eat and many places for them to shelter and raise their young. The structure of rainforests and coral reefs depends on living things. Trees form the giant "jungle gym" that supports a rainforest, while a coral reef is supported by the empty skeletons of dead coral animals. Rainforests and coral reefs have both been growing on our planet for millions of years.

Superforests

Rainforests cover only 6 percent of Earth's surface, but they are home to more than half of all the different kinds of plants and animals on Earth. Sadly, an area of rainforest the size of a soccer field is being destroyed every second.

Coral reefs are home to about one third of all the different kinds of fish in the world. The fish usually have very bright colors. Their bright patterns and markings help them recognize other fish like themselves.

Glossary

acid
A chemical substance that breaks rocks down to form new minerals. Rainwater contains some carbonic acid, which is a weak acid consisting of carbon dioxide dissolved in water.

atmosphere
A blanket of gases around a massive object such as a planet, held in place by the pull of the object's gravity.

continent
One of the seven large areas of land on Earth. Earth's continents are Africa, Antarctica, Asia, Australia, Europe, North America, and South America.

continental drift
The way the continents slowly move around on the surface of the globe because of powerful forces deep inside Earth.

coral reef
An underwater structure made up of the skeletons of dead animals called corals, with living corals growing on top.

crystal
A hard, glassy-looking object made of minerals. Crystals have smooth faces, straight edges, and symmetrical corners.

cumulus cloud
A fluffy, white, cauliflower-shaped cloud that forms at low levels in good weather. This cloud is named after the Latin word for "heap up," which is *cumulo*.

cumulonimbus cloud
A tall thundercloud, with a flat, dark base. It brings heavy rain, thunder, lightning, and hailstorms.

earthquake
A shaking of the ground caused by sudden movements of the rocks deep underground. The biggest earthquakes are triggered by the movement of Earth's plates.

fault line
A long crack in the rocks in Earth's crust where blocks of rock slip past one another.

fossil
The remains or traces of living things from the past, preserved in the rocks.

geometric shape
A three-dimensional shape with a regular, symmetrical structure. Crystals form in one of seven geometric shapes (such as cubic or hexagonal) according to the arrangement of the molecules (tiny particles) inside them.

gravity
An invisible force of attraction between objects. The gravity of massive objects, such as Earth, is very strong. Earth's gravity stops things on its surface from flying off into space by pulling them toward its center.

hot spring

A place where hot water, full of minerals, bubbles to the surface. The water is heated by hot rocks under the ground.

limestone

A layered rock made mainly from the mineral calcite, which is the main ingredient in seashells. Some limestone rocks are made from the shells of ancient sea creatures; others are made from chemicals.

meteors

Tiny chunks of rock or ice falling from space toward Earth. Many meteors burn up in Earth's atmosphere, but if they reach the surface they are called meteorites.

mineral

A hard, natural substance in the ground that makes up rocks.

planet

A large ball of rock, metal, or gas that orbits (goes around) a star. Earth is a planet that orbits the Sun, our nearest star.

polar lands

The frozen lands around Earth's North and South poles. The polar lands at the top of the planet are called the Arctic, and the lands at the bottom of the planet are called Antarctica.

rainforest

A thick forest with tall trees that is warm and wet all year long. Rainforests grow around Earth's middle, near its "waist."

reflection

The bouncing back of light from a surface.

seasons

Regular changes in the pattern of the weather throughout the year. Some places have four seasons (spring, summer, fall, and winter); other places have two seasons (summer and winter, or wet and dry seasons).

senses

The physical abilities that animals use to find out about their surroundings. Animals often have five senses: sight, hearing, smell, touch, and taste.

spring tide

A very high or a very low tide that happens twice every month.

static electricity

A form of electricity produced when certain materials are rubbed together. Lightning is a huge spark of static electricity.

stratus cloud

A very low-level, flat, shapeless cloud that can cover the entire sky. On the ground, stratus clouds form mist or fog. They often give long periods of rain.

tsunami

A giant sea wave caused by an underwater earthquake.

vent

An opening in the ground through which volcanic materials (such as hot, liquid rocks from deep underground) escape to Earth's surface.

water vapor

The invisible gas that water turns into when it is heated.

Index

The Publisher would like to thank the following for permission to reproduce their material. Every care has been taken to trace copyright holders. However, if there have been unintentional omissions or failure to trace copyright holders, we apologize and will, if informed, endeavor to make corrections in any future edition.

Pages 4 Shutterstock/ixpert; 6 Shutterstock/marcokenya; 7 Corbis/Stephen Dalton; 9 Corbis/Frans Lanting; 10 Shutterstock/bierchen; 12 Shutterstock/axel2001; 13 Corbis/Roger Ressmeyer; 14 Science Photo Library/NOAA; 16 Shutterstock/Krill Smirnov; 17 Shutterstock/RZ-photo; 19 Shutterstock/Robert Fesus; 20 Shutterstock/Krill Smirnov; 21 Shutterstock/magdanatka; 22 Corbis/Richard Nowitz; 24 Corbis/Doug Meek; 25 Science Photo Library/Javier Trueba/MSF; 26 Shutterstock/kamuan; 29 Shutterstock/Vlad61.